The Big
STORM
P9-CAP-685

This book is dedicated to my mother,
JEANETTE GROSNEY BLOCK,
and to the memory of my grandfather,
ARON GROSNEY.

R.T.

To Jenny

M.K.

Kids Can Press Ltd. acknowledges with appreciation the assistance of the Canada Council and the Ontario Arts Council in the production of this book.

CANADIAN CATALOGUING IN PUBLICATION DATA

Tregebov, Rhea, 1953–
The big storm

ISBN 1-55074-081-4

I. Kovalski, Maryann. II. Title.

PS8589.R44B5 1992 jC813'.54 C91-095404-6
PZ7.T74Bi 1992

Kids Can Press Ltd.
585 1/2 Bloor Street West
Toronto, Ontario, Canada
M6G 1K5.

Designed by N.R. Jackson
Typeset by Cybergraphics Co. Inc.
Printed and bound in Hong Kong by
Colorcraft Ltd.

PA 92 0 9 8 7 6 5 4 3 2 1

written by Rhea Tregebov
illustrated by Maryann Kovalski

Kids Can Press Ltd.
Toronto

Once upon a time, there was a little girl called Jeanette and a cat named Kitty Doyle. Jeanette and Kitty Doyle lived above the delicatessen, where every morning was a busy morning.

DELI · GROS NEY · CAFE
DELI · GROSNEY · CAFE
DELI · CAF

In the kitchen, Momma made borscht and gefilte fish. At the front of the store, Poppa wrapped and sold herring and pickles.

Jeanette's big brothers hurried back and forth helping with the deliveries. It was Jeanette's job to sweep up so the floor was clean as a whistle for the customers.

Kitty Doyle worked too. She was not only a beautiful cat, she was clever and she was the best mouser on Selkirk Avenue.

At Grosney's Delicatessen, not even the whisker of a mouse could be found.

Kitty Doyle had another job. Every morning she walked
Jeanette to school and every afternoon she walked her home.

"Jeanette," Poppa said one morning, "don't forget an extra sweater. The radio says more snow."

"I'm all bundled up, Poppa! Come on, Kitty Doyle. It's time for school."

Kitty Doyle ran fancy circles around Jeanette as they walked to Selkirk and Salter. Aberdeen School was just around the corner.

"This is as far as you go," Jeanette said. "Don't stay outside to play. Go straight home! I'll see you after school."

Poppa's radio had been right. When school let out, a thick quilt of fresh snow covered the school yard. The children couldn't wait to make forts and snowmen. By the time the snowball fights were done, Jeanette and her friend Polly were soaked.

“Come to my house,” Polly said. “You can dry off there. My mom is making her special latkes. They’ll be ready by the time we get there.”

“Latkes!” Jeanette could almost taste them. Polly’s mother had a secret recipe — no one else’s were quite as good.

"Leo," Jeanette called to her brother across the school yard, "tell Poppa I'm going to Polly's for latkes."

"Okay, kiddo," Leo called back. "Wish you could bring some home for me."

As the girls hurried to Polly's house, the snow began to fall more heavily.

The frost on the kitchen windows was so thick you could hardly see out. Jeanette was taking the last crunchy bite when she suddenly remembered.

"Polly! I forgot all about Kitty Doyle!" Jeanette jumped down from her chair and began pulling on her boots.

"Maybe she just went home," said Polly.

"Not Kitty Doyle. She wouldn't leave until I got there."

Before Polly could say another word, Jeanette was out the door.

How could she have forgotten? Kitty Doyle would never have forgotten about her.

By the time she reached the school, Jeanette was almost out of breath, but she wouldn't stop. Flora Avenue was dark and empty and wide.

A shabby tomcat yowled as Jeanette ran past the school yard. "That is not Kitty Doyle," she thought. "Not my Kitty Doyle." Round the last corner to Selkirk Avenue.... Nothing there.

She started up the street, but at the third building she stopped.

In a narrow alley Jeanette saw a little bump in the snow. She ran up and brushed off the snow with her thick woollen mitten.

"I knew you'd wait for me. I knew you wouldn't go home alone."

Jeanette tucked Kitty Doyle deep in her coat. "Be all right," she whispered. "Please be all right. Don't be sick." Kitty Doyle was very still.

When they got to the store, there was milk heating on the stove. Gently Jeanette wrapped Kitty Doyle in Poppa's sweater. Then she took honey from a jar and added it to the pot. She poured the sweet warm milk into the cat's special bowl.

"Jeanette?" Poppa asked, taking off his apron, "Jeanette, what is wrong with the cat?"

Jeanette started to cry. "I got soaked in a snowball fight and I went to Polly's for latkes. And we sat in the kitchen eating and eating, and Kitty Doyle waited and waited for me in the cold...."

"Take off your wet things, Jeanette," Poppa said. "Go warm up by the stove."

Jeanette knelt beside Kitty Doyle and let the cat lick the milk from her fingers. As Poppa and Jeanette watched, Kitty Doyle finished the bowl of milk.

"That's good, she's eating. Now you come and eat something too."

Poppa brought two steaming bowls of chicken soup and set them on the counter. Jeanette sat in front of hers and put her hands around the warm bowl.

Kitty Doyle carefully washed each paw.

“A cat who washes its paws is not a sick cat.”

“Are you sure, Poppa?” Jeanette asked.

“Am I sure? Sure I’m sure!”

After Kitty Doyle had washed her face, Jeanette settled the cat into her lap. Then Jeanette and Poppa ate their soup and listened, as the streetcars rumbled down Selkirk Avenue and the storm grew quiet.

The only sound was Kitty Doyle, purring.